Sword

and

Crown

Dragon Riders of Osnen Book 12

RICHARD FIERCE

Dragonfire Press

Copyright © 2022 Richard Fierce

Cover design by germancreative.

Cover art by Nimesh Niyomal

ISBN: 978-1-9583544-09-4

CONTENTS

1

I stepped out of the dovecote and glanced along the street, heaving a sigh. There was still no word from Anesko. I'd sent him a missive after finding the Carver and gave him some of the details, but I hadn't heard back from him. That had been a week ago.

Now that I knew there was a band of dragon slayers roaming the land, I'd gained a heightened concern for Sion. It was difficult to kill a dragon, but the slayers made killing the king's look easy. I suspected they had a powerful sorcerer with them.

Don't worry, Sion said. *Magic or not, no one will sneak up on me without notice.*

I'd like to agree with you, but the evidence says otherwise.

The royal riders are weak. They lie around the castle all day, lazy and growing fat. You and I have seen more enemies in our short time together than they have combined.

I smiled as she rumbled on. She had a valid point, but I had no desire to face dragon slayers without Maren or Katori at my side. I'd learned long ago that the best weapon against a sorcerer was another sorcerer. I waited for a lull in the crowd and stepped onto the street, following the flow of people heading east toward the main gates.

I wish Anesko would call us back to the Citadel already. It feels like it's been an eternity since I saw Maren.

He wants you to learn from your mistakes. Have you done so?

Yes.

Sion remained silent.

Well, I think so.

I do not.

What do you mean?

We left the school and immediately tracked down the Carver. Your thoughts haven't strayed to what you've done once since we've been gone.

I grimaced. Being bonded to a dragon had a host of benefits, but there were a few cons, too. Such as having your thoughts read. Sometimes it was a good thing, but every once in a while, it would be nice to have some privacy. Truthfully, I was avoiding thinking about the events in Ilok. T'Mere lost his life because of me. The less I thought about that, the easier it was to go about my day.

A dragon rider is approaching, Sion said.

I looked at the sky and squinted, but I couldn't

tell who it was.

Someone from the Citadel?

No. I've never seen them before.

The hope that Master Anesko had sent someone, specifically Maren, to retrieve me was quickly dashed. But if it wasn't a rider from the Citadel, then it had to be one of the king's men. Why would the king send someone to Tiradale, though?

I watched until the dragon came into view. It was a vibrant sapphire color. A banner affixed to a pole on the saddle flapped in the wind. I was right. The banner bore the king's crest. The dragon spiraled down and landed outside the city, near Sion's location. I frowned and walked faster, pushing through the crowd.

What's going on? I asked.

The rider is requesting your presence.

I'm on my way.

What could the king want with me? To gloat some more over my suspension? Possibly, as he was that petty, but he didn't know Anesko's punishment was temporary. I reached the gates and left the city, then turned right and followed the wall until I saw Sion. The blue dragon waited a few feet from her, its tail swishing back and forth. The creature seemed restless.

The rider slipped out of the saddle and landed gracefully on the ground. His bearing was one of importance, and his hawkish features added a layer of seriousness to his demeanor.

"Eldwin Baines?" he asked as I approached.

"Maybe. Who are you?"

"Captain Rouzet of His Majesty's private guard. Is this your dragon?"

I studied the man's appearance. The only hair on his entire head was a thin horseshoe mustache that stretched down from his upper lip to his chin. It was meticulously groomed. His eyes were blue, and he had a small scar on his neck that disappeared behind his right ear.

"Yes, she is my dragon," I replied.

"Then you *are* Eldwin Baines?"

"That's me."

"You're under arrest by order of the king."

"Arrest? For what?"

"Theft from the royal treasury."

"I didn't steal anything. The king gave that money to the Citadel to use for our investigation."

"It's not a matter to be contested," the rider said. "You need to come with me." He glanced at Sion.

"By force if necessary."

Let him try, Sion growled.

"That won't be necessary. We'll go with you willingly."

"Good. Do you need to collect any belongings? I can escort you."

For a moment, I entertained the thought of leading him on a wild chase through the city, but common sense prevailed and I shook my head.

"I'm ready to go when you are."

"Very well."

He lifted his right hand into the air and traced a symbol while muttering something under his breath. Sion tensed.

"What are you doing?" I asked.

The rider finished his spell and turned to face me. "Ensuring your cooperation. If your dragon tries to flee, I will go where you go."

I should chomp his head from his body, Sion bristled.

Let's wait and see what the king plans to do. If things go wrong, you are free to chomp all the heads you want.

Promise?

I rolled my eyes and climbed up her shoulder, seating myself in the saddle.

What did he do to you?

He's tethered himself to me with magic. If I get too far away from him, he'll be pulled to where I am.

That could be interesting, I said.

It's annoying, she huffed.

The rider climbed onto his dragon's back, and the beast took to the air. Sion stretched her wings out wide and followed the rider's lead, easily catching up. She positioned herself to the left of the blue dragon and we flew in silence for a long while. I considered how I would have responded months ago. I'd changed a lot since my first days at the school.

The familiar terrain of the Citadel came into view, but we continued past, heading east toward Istral, the capital of Osnen. I was curious what Erling thought to accomplish by arresting me. I had no money to pay him back, but I suspected that wasn't truly what he wanted. He hated me because I was a lowborn, and the fact I had married his daughter was probably salt on the wound.

Maren had chosen me over him, after all.

The Citadel was gone from my view when the

king's rider waved his arm to get my attention. I looked at him curiously, and he motioned for me to land. I nodded.

Take us down, I told Sion.

The blue dragon descended, and Sion kept a close but safe proximity as she did the same. We landed on the bank of a wide river. Judging by our location, I assumed it was the Colos. Its source was the melting ice at the western end of the Gracena Mountains.

I dismounted and stretched. The rider was kneeling beside his dragon, his expression one of concern. I approached slowly.

"What's going on?"

"She doesn't feel well. We'll stay here until she can fly again. It shouldn't be too long."

I didn't know what to say, so I walked to the edge of the river and splashed some water on my face. It was freezing, and I involuntarily sucked in a sharp breath.

I think we're being watched, Sion said.

Yeah, by His Highness's lackey.

No, someone else. Someone ... unseen.

I wiped the water from my eyes and looked at her. She was staring intently back the way we'd come. I walked over to stand beside her and watched the horizon. There was nothing out of the ordinary, but Sion had never been wrong before.

Stay alert, I said.

Captain Rouzet's focus was on his dragon, and I suspected if Sion and I snuck away, he likely wouldn't notice. It was a tempting thought, but I didn't want to earn the ire of the captain. He was just following orders. Besides that, I was morbidly curious to see what Erling had planned for me. So long as I had a means of escape from the castle, I wasn't too worried. I didn't know my way around the palace well, which meant my escape would likely be hasty.

The minutes turned to hours, and the captain's dragon showed no signs of getting any better. Evening was closing in. I retrieved an apple from Sion's saddle and took a bite. Captain Rouzet left his dragon and walked over to me.

"We're going to have to camp here for the night. She's not feeling well enough to fly yet."

I'd been expecting that news, so I nodded.

"It won't be the first time I've slept under the stars," I said. "I'm sure this won't be the last, either."

2

The wind ruffled my cloak as I stood at the edge of the cliff face. There were no clouds in the sky overhead, and the light of the sun warmed my skin comfortingly. The clear ocean water stretched out into eternity, or so it seemed. I looked down. The cliff rose a few hundred feet above the ocean, and I could see jagged rocks sticking up from the water's surface when the waves weren't crashing against them.

I could also see caves. The dark alcoves dotted the side of the cliff, all varying sizes. Something had called me here, and I felt as though this had happened before. Whispers danced on the wind, the words just out of reach. I strained to hear them, but they remained elusive.

Something flashed at the opening of one of the caves and I watched expectantly, waiting to see what it was, but nothing revealed itself. After a long moment, my impatience got the better of me and I began scaling down the side of the cliff. I skipped the first few openings and stopped at the one I'd seen movement at, carefully placing my foot on the ledge and pushing myself to safety.

In the back of my mind, I wondered where Sion was, but it didn't seem important at the moment. My purpose for being here was a higher priority … whatever that purpose was. I rested my hand on the hilt of my sword and stepped into the shadows of the cave. A scraping sound echoed off the walls.

"Hello?"

Why are you here, human?

"I … don't know. Something drew me here."

You are not welcome in this place. You must leave.

"Where would I go?"

Anywhere but here.

"Are you one of the Wild Ones?" I asked.

The hidden creature growled, the sound vibrating the surrounding air. I tightened the grip on my hilt, but I didn't unsheathe my blade. The last thing I wanted was to anger the beast, and considering it hid in the shadows, I doubted I could escape before it attacked unseen.

How did you know to find us here?

"I don't know what you mean. Who are you?"

I heard the creature approaching, and my muscles tensed. Two large glowing eyes appeared amid the shadows.

I am a Wild One.

The words entered my mind as a gentle whisper, but I knew there was nothing gentle behind those eyes. The intensity of them made me swallow and weigh my words.

"Show yourself."

The eyes drew closer, and I walked backward,

stopping when my heel scraped over the ledge into the open air. The eyes continued to come nearer, and then they stopped at the edge of the darkness.

You are either brave or very foolish.

"A little of both," I said, forcing a nervous smile.

The creature snorted. *I smell your fear, human. There is nothing brave about your kind. You consume and destroy, and you do it all for nothing!*

Warm air washed over me, and then I was free falling. I watched in mute terror as the cliff seemed to grow, and I was certain I was going to land on the jagged rocks in the water.

Eldwin.

Someone was calling my name. I could hear it over the whipping wind. Was it the beast from the cave? I scanned the cliff face, desperately hoping the creature would help me.

Eldwin.

"Help!" I screamed.

Eldwin.

I jerked violently, and my eyes snapped open. A nightmare. It had all been a dream. I sat up and looked around. Captain Rouzet was asleep beside his dragon. The cooking fire was long dead, and the sky was still dark. Sion was awake, though, and her gaze rested on me.

It's about time, she huffed.

What do you mean?

I was calling your name. Were you ignoring me?

No, of course not. I was dreaming of the Whispering Cliffs again. It seemed so real.

Forget that. Someone's coming.

I got to my feet and grabbed my sword belt, peering into the night.

I don't see anything.

Neither do I, but I know they are approaching.

They?

There are multiple scents in my nose. One of them is using magic, too.

My mind immediately went to the dragon slayers, but why would they be out here? Were they tracking us? And if so, why? I strapped my belt on and unsheathed my blade, then hurried over to the captain, gently shaking his shoulder. The *shing* of metal sounded, and I felt the sharp tip of a dagger pressed against my neck.

"What are you doing?" Rouzet asked.

"We've got company," I whispered, nodding toward Sion.

Rouzet's eyes flicked in the same direction she was staring. He withdrew the dagger and stood up.

"I don't see anyone."

"Neither do I, but Sion's never been wrong

before. She says someone is using magic, and I suspect they're using it to conceal themselves."

"Friends of yours from the Citadel?"

"Not likely."

Rouzet looked at his dragon and placed a hand on her neck.

"She's not getting any better. I don't know why."

I wanted to tell him about the dragon slayers, but I doubted he would believe me. I wouldn't have believed it either if I hadn't seen it with my own eyes.

"Let her rest," I said. "The three of us can handle it." I hoped I sounded more confident than I felt.

"Why are you still here? You and your dragon could have fled already."

"I've thought about it more than once," I admitted. "But I don't desire to be at the other end of the king's wrath."

"He called for your arrest. I doubt there's much more you could do to earn his fury."

I shrugged.

"We can't leave your dragon behind, so we need a plan. Any ideas?"

"I don't know if it will fool them," Rouzet said, "but we could pretend to be asleep and surprise them when they show themselves."

I had the same thought. "That might work. If it doesn't, thanks for not dragging me from Ilok in chains."

"That's not my preferred method." Rouzet smiled. We clasped each other's arms at the elbow and then took our positions. He remained near his dragon, and I sat beside Sion, my back pressed against her foreleg. I set my sword on the ground but kept my hand on the hilt.

I doubt we'll be able to take them alive, I told Sion. *We'll have to make quick work of the sorcerer.*

None of them will escape with their lives, she promised.

I closed my eyes to thin slits and waited. It wasn't long before I heard a rustling sound. There was no one in sight, but it was obvious there were several people present. Sion's leg tensed under me.

Hold, I said.

Her bulk moved suddenly, and I turned my head just in time to see her mouth snap closed, two legs dangling from her mouth. It must have been the sorcerer because the illusion faded and half a dozen people became visible. They all wore a mix of plate armor and chainmail, and they wielded weapons that glowed faintly, reminding me of the ones Maren and I had found in the Terran monastery.

One of them, a brute of a man, held a spear and he jabbed the head of it into Sion's chest. It pierced her scales, and she roared in anger and pain, jumping up. I fell backward, banging my head on the ground. Waves of pain washed over me, but I pushed through them and scrambled to my feet. I engaged the man who'd stabbed her, the back of my skull burning like fire.

He parried my strike, and it surprised me when my blade didn't cut through the wooden pole of his spear. From my periphery, I saw Rouzet attack one of the others. He was well trained with a blade, but his opponent was just as skilled. I turned my attention back to my enemy and grabbed onto the haft of his spear with my left hand. Darkness overwhelmed my thoughts, and for a brief moment, I was back at the monastery trying to kill Sion.

I roared and pushed the man back, releasing the cursed weapon. The brute stumbled, but he didn't go down. He pointed the end of his spear at me and charged. I smacked it aside with my sword and dropped low, swinging the blade at his legs. The sharp steel cut through his pants and opened a gash in his flesh, but if he felt pain, he didn't show it. I rose and saw there were more enemies than before.

Sion was heaving deep breaths, and Rouzet was now surrounded. The man with the spear ran toward Rouzet's dragon and stabbed the beast, driving the weapon so far into her that only a small portion of the haft was visible. No sound escaped the dragon, but she shuddered and went still. I knew then that these people, these dragon slayers, were responsible for her unexplained illness.

Rouzet screamed as they cut him down. Sion and I were going to die if we didn't escape. I sheathed my blade and climbed up Sion's shoulder, throwing myself into the saddle.

Go!

She stretched her wings out and leaped into the air. A few flaps of her wings put some distance between us and the murderous maniacs, and I looked over my shoulder to see if they were pursuing us. Rouzet's body flew off the ground and crashed into those who slew him, knocking them aside. I wondered what kind of sorcery was at work, and I remembered he had bound himself magically to Sion. His corpse dragged on the ground until Sion ascended higher, and then he dangled oddly below us.

No more of that, Sion said, and then Rouzet's body fell to the ground and I lost sight of it among the shadows.

We need to get to the Citadel.

I won't make it that far.

Why not?

I've been poisoned.

3

The words made little sense for a moment.

Poisoned? How do you know?

I feel it flowing through my blood. It must have been on the spear that stabbed me.

Sion was struggling to continue flapping her wings, and I could feel her heaving in breaths.

Land, I urged. *Exerting yourself is going to make it worse.*

We must put some distance between us and them, Sion replied.

I looked back, but it was impossible to make out any details in the dark. For a brief moment, I felt saddened at Captain Rouzet's death. I didn't know him, but he seemed like an honorable man despite working for the king.

I think they poisoned Rouzet's dragon, too.

Probably, Sion huffed.

She was straining so much I could feel it through the bond. I was beginning to worry this was going to end badly, but I pushed the thought to the back of my mind. We flew in silence for a fair distance before I decided we were safely ahead of our enemies.

Take us down.

I expected Sion to argue with me, but she descended and landed roughly in a field. I could see the dark silhouette of a building and realized it was a farm.

How far are we from the Citadel? I asked.

Several miles.

Sion collapsed tiredly onto the ground, her mouth open. Her tongue lolled out onto the dirt and she panted heavily. Fear squirmed in the pit of my stomach. It had been a while since I'd felt it this intensely, and I did not miss the sensation. I swallowed the lump in my throat and rested a hand against Sion's snout.

You should go, she said.

I'm not leaving you here alone.

I'll be fine.

Not with those dragon slayers roaming about.

There's nothing you can do for me. You need to get help.

She was right, but I didn't want to leave her behind. I clenched my jaw, anger at the slayers overcoming my fear.

Dawn isn't far off, I said. *Once the sun comes up, I'll go. At the very least, you'll be able to see them coming in the daylight.*

I did fear she might not survive that long, but I stopped the thought before it crossed into the bond. I drew my sword and sat down beside her, laying the blade across my lap. Sion didn't say anything. I pushed comforting emotions through the bond, hoping they would ease her discomfort a little.

Eventually, her breathing steadied and she fell asleep. I stayed awake, not that I could sleep even if I wanted to. My mind was racing. Dragon slayers. Here, in Osnen. Why were they here? What did they hope to accomplish? There were too many questions and no answers. Perhaps Anesko would have some knowledge of them.

I stood up, trying to be as quiet as possible, and trekked across the field back the way we'd come. I didn't see or hear anything aside from the nighttime sounds of animals and insects. Sion had killed the sorcerer, but that didn't make the others any less dangerous. Their weapons were just like the ones I'd found in the Terran monastery, designed to kill dragons. I'd assumed the monks had died out, but perhaps they were still around.

These people didn't seem to be monks, but it was possible they followed the same teachings. I returned to Sion's side and stared at her as she slept. There were also the dreams that haunted me every night. The last one had been the strangest yet. The creature had confirmed it was a Wild One, whatever that was, and it had attacked me. At least, I think it had. I certainly didn't throw myself out of the cave.

The hours seemed to stretch longer than was possible, but finally, the sun crested over the horizon. We were in the middle of a farming field that was freshly plowed for planting. To the left, a portion was sectioned off and already fertilized. Ahead, the door of the farm creaked open and three men stepped out. One was older, clearly the father of the other two. They stopped and stared wide-eyed. I sheathed my sword and strolled toward them, smiling.

"Morning," I greeted. "I'm sorry to frighten you, but my dragon is injured. We're on our way to the Citadel and she was forced to land here a few hours ago."

The father kept his eyes on Sion, ignoring me until I was only a few feet away. His boys huddled behind him, and I thought they looked young for their height.

"You cannot stay here," the man said.

"We don't intend to. As I said, we're going to the Citadel."

"You need to leave now, please. I don't want any trouble."

"There's no trouble," I replied. "I mean you no harm."

"I'm not afraid of you. The riders have never raised a hand against us, despite the rumors others may mutter. No, good sir, I am afraid of those hunting you."

"Who are you talking about?" I knew, but I wanted him to confirm it.

"They came through here a few days ago. They look like mercenaries, but it isn't money that drives them. It's evil. I heard them talking. They are here to kill dragons."

So it *was* the dragon slayers he had seen. I nodded.

"I ran into them last night. Do you know where they came from?"

"I'm afraid not," the man answered. "After I heard their talk of killing dragons, I locked myself inside the house until they left. Anyone who seeks to harm a dragon is no friend of mine."

It was good to know that there were still some people who hadn't cast us aside.

"My dragon is too hurt to fly. I need to get to the Citadel, but she needs to rest."

"I'm sorry, but you must both leave now. I can't risk the safety of my family. If those people come back and find out I aided you, I'm certain they'll kill us all."

He was probably right about that. If they were hunting dragons, they wouldn't hesitate to kill innocent bystanders. Still, Sion wasn't able to travel, not without making it worse on herself.

"Please," I begged. "Let her stay where she is. I'll return shortly, and we'll get her out of here. I'll make sure you and your family are safe."

I really couldn't guarantee that. Our ranks were stretched thin already, but I would ask Anesko to do what he could, even if it was just putting up some wards around the farm. The man met my eyes, and we stared at one another in silence.

"Fine," he relented. "But if they come while you

are gone, I cannot help your dragon."

"I'm not asking you to. She can hold her own."

The man grunted. "You better hurry, then."

"Thank you. You, uh, wouldn't happen to have a horse I could borrow?" I smiled again.

"Bah! Behind the house in the stable. Take the brown one. The black one is too old to be ridden."

I bowed to the man and rushed back to Sion. She was awake, but she was sluggish, and her thoughts and emotions came through the bond in a disjointed mess.

I'm going to get help. Stay here and try not to move. And don't bother the farmer.

Sion's eyelids blinked lazily.

Goodbye, Eldwin.

I'll be back.

I ran around the back of the farm and found the brown horse in the stable, just as the man said. I'd only ridden a horse a few times, but I remembered the basics. There was a saddle hanging on the wall but I decided not to didn't bother with it. The quicker I reached the Citadel, the quicker Sion would get help.

I led the horse out of the stall and used a wooden crate to climb onto the animal, then urged her onward. She thundered through the field and onto the road. I glanced back. Sion lay still. I turned my gaze ahead and urged the horse to go faster, praying Sion didn't die.

4

A mile from the school, the horse collapsed from exhaustion. I continued on foot, running until my strength gave out. When I entered the courtyard of the school, my leg muscles burned so fiercely that I couldn't take another step. I staggered and fell, and everything became disoriented. Several faces flashed before me, including Master Katori's.

"Eldwin? What are you doing here? Where's Sion?"

I opened my mouth and said the only thing I had the strength to muster which was, "Anesko."

The next thing I knew, someone splashed water on my face. The coldness of it forced the exhaustion away, and I saw Master Katori standing over me, a bucket in her hands.

"Give him some room," Anesko said as he strode over to me. "You aren't supposed to be here," he said sternly. I could see the concern in his eyes despite his tone.

"I need help," I rasped. "Sion's been poisoned by dragon slayers."

A collective gasp arose from those gathered.

"Bring him inside," Anesko instructed. "Quickly."

Several of my fellow riders picked me up and carried me into the school. Once inside, they took me to the infirmary. I tried to tell everyone I was fine, but no one was listening. Anesko entered last and commanded everyone to leave.

"I don't need medical attention," I said, pushing myself onto the edge of the cot they had placed me on.

"I know. I brought you here to keep prying ears away. Tell me everything."

I nodded and relayed all that had happened since I'd left the Citadel, explaining as fast as I could without leaving out important details. Sion was waiting for me, and I knew that every moment without help was another second closer to disaster.

"Sion is still at the farm now?" Anesko asked.

"Yes. Please help her," I begged.

"We will do everything we can. Can you walk?"

"Yes. I feel better now that I've rested a little. And the water in my face helped." I smiled.

"Good. Let's go help Sion."

I stood up and my leg muscles flared with pain, but I ignored the discomfort and walked with Anesko. People were milling around in the hall and he began issuing orders. Within minutes, we were back in the courtyard and several riders were ready to depart. Anesko and I mounted his dragon, and we left the school and flew to where I had left Sion.

Her massive red body was easy to see as we approached, and the riders landed on the outer edge of the farming field to keep from tearing up the crops. The farmer and his sons retreated into their home. In all the chaos, I hadn't even thought to ask for Maren to come with us. Master Katori was present, which brought me some relief. She dismounted from her dragon, one that she had taken from the Citadel. Her dragon had died when magic failed, and it pained me every time I thought about it. It was partially my fault, after all.

Katori rushed to where Sion lay and knelt in front of her. I leaped from the saddle to the ground and joined her. I could still feel her presence in the bond, but she felt weak.

"The wound is bad," Katori said, pressing her fingertips around it gently. "Something is keeping it from healing. What happened?"

I looked over my shoulder at Anesko as he approached, unsure of what exactly he wanted to share with everyone.

"We were attacked, and she was poisoned," I answered.

Katori leaned in close and sniffed the wound, wrinkling her nose. "It's going to kill her if we don't get her a cure," she said. "Get my bag from the saddle."

I did as she asked, rushing to her borrowed dragon and returning with a bag that clinked with glass bottles. She took it and began pulling out vials, laying them aside. She picked one and poured it on the wound. Sion stirred, her eyelids flickering, but she didn't wake. We waited to see if anything happened, but Sion's presence in the bond remained the same.

"I don't sense any change in her," I said.

Katori opened another vial, again applying it to Sion's wound. We waited, but as with the first one, there was no noticeable difference. She tried a third, and a fourth, all with the same results. After she spent all the vials, Katori looked at me and Anesko.

"I have done all I can, but nothing has helped. I do not know what else to try."

That was not what I wanted to hear. I looked at Anesko.

"Master Katori is the most knowledgeable about treating dragons, so I'm afraid I'm of no help here. Is there anything else you can think of?"

Katori shook her head. "Whatever this poison is made from, it is potent. I have seen nothing like it before."

"We were attacked by dragon slayers," I said lowly.

"Eldwin," Anesko hissed, glancing behind us. The other riders seemed oblivious to what I said, so I wasn't worried.

"She already knows."

"What did these people look like?" Katori asked. "Were they Terran?"

"No, they weren't Terran. They weren't from Osnen, either. It was dark when they attacked, so I didn't get a good look at them, but their armor was not like anything I'd seen before. They're definitely foreign."

"Valguaard?" Anesko asked.

"No. They are the same ones who killed the king's riders."

"Dragon slayers," Katori said, shaking her head. "Remember the weapons you found in the temple I took you to?"

"How could I forget?"

"Those are the only dragon slayers I know of, but they have been dead for many years."

"I fought one of them and when I touched his weapon, it felt the same as when I held the sword from the temple. It was enchanted with dark magic. I have no doubt of that."

"How many were there?" Anesko asked.

"Six at first, then more appeared. A dozen, maybe? Sion killed one of them, a sorcerer. She cloaked their movement, which is probably how they caught the king's riders unaware."

"Any ideas?" Anesko asked Katori. She shook her head.

"We can't let her die," I said, placing a hand on Sion's snout. A thought came to me suddenly, but it wasn't one I liked. "The Assembly. They fought against dragon slayers. Perhaps they have a cure."

Anesko frowned. "It's possible, but Sion doesn't look like she can walk, let alone fly. How will you get her there?"

That was a question I didn't have the answer to.

"Can another dragon carry her?" I asked.

"The distance is too far," Anesko said. "It would take a toll on any dragon, and that would mean more stops to rest. It's not ideal."

"There is a way," Katori said. "You can travel by magic, but I do not know where the Assembly is. You would have to forge your way there, but I can open the door."

"What about Sion?"

"The magic will allow her to go, but she will need to enter the portal on her own. Once inside, the magic will do the rest."

"She can do that," I said, hoping I was right.

"It will take a lot of energy to travel that far," Katori warned. "I do not know if I have the strength to hold the portal for long."

I reached through the bond and gently touched Sion's presence.

Sion, can you hear me?

Eldwin, her voice was frail.

We're going to get you some help, but I need you to take a few steps. Can you do that?

I can try.

"We're ready," I said to Katori.

"Very well. I will open the portal, but you will need to tell the magic where to take you. Once the portal closes on this end, there is nothing I can do to help you if something goes wrong."

"What could go wrong?" I asked.

"Many things, but do not consider that. Just focus on your destination."

I nodded. Katori rose to her feet and began speaking the words to her spell, muttering them under her breath as she stood with her hands facing palm outward. The hair on my arms stood on end, and the air in front of Sion rippled. A large tear opened, and on the other side, I could see a swirling black and purple abyss.

Sion, I need you to enter the portal.

Her eyes fluttered open, but she didn't budge.

Get up, I urged. *We don't have much time.*

I can't move, she replied. *My body will not obey me. I do not have the strength.*

Use mine.

I opened the bond fully. She hesitated, but I pushed my energy through the bond, flooding her end with my vigor. Sion latched onto it and drew it within herself, pulling more than I expected. She lifted herself and lurched forward into the portal. I followed right behind her and tried to envision the forest where the Assembly dwelled, but my mind was clouded. Sion had taken most of my strength, and I fought to stay conscious, but everything went dark.

5

When I opened my eyes, Sion and I were floating in the magical tunnel. I looked all around, but there was no sign of the opening. How long had I been out? It was impossible to know. Sion was beside me, and I reached out and grabbed hold of her hind leg. I tried my best not to panic concerning our predicament, but it was difficult.

I took a deep breath and closed my eyes, picturing the black stone walls of the Temple of the Bond. I hoped Katori's magic worked. My stomach dropped, and I opened my eyes to see the swirling passageway speed past my vision so quickly it was nothing more than a blur of black and purple.

I blinked, and suddenly I was lying on the ground looking up at the blue sky. A few white clouds were visible, and I rolled my head to the side. Sion was here, too. It had worked. I sat up and saw the temple in front of us, which spurred me to action.

You're going to be fine, I told Sion.

She didn't respond. I got on my feet and hurried up the steps of the temple. Just as I was about to push on the door, it swung open. Nemryth the Dark stepped out, her gaze looking beyond me to where Sion was.

"What are you doing here?" she asked. "And what's wrong with your bonded?"

"I need your help. Sion's been poisoned."

Nemryth turned her attention to me. "Poisoned how?"

"It's a long story, but we were attacked by dragon slayers. They—"

"I know of them," she interrupted. "Come inside. Tyrval will take care of Sion."

Nemryth went back into the temple and I followed her. The interior of the temple mirrored the exterior in that it was composed of black stone. Unlike human temples, there were no tapestries on the walls and no rugs lining the floor. The atmosphere resembled that of a cave. It was dim, slightly humid, and held the scent of aged parchment.

"Are you saying you knew there were dragon slayers in Osnen and you didn't inform the Order?"

"They only recently arrived," Nemryth answered defensively. "Risod has been trying to track them down, but they remain … elusive."

"It should be easier to find them now," I said. "Sion killed the sorcerer that was with them. I'm sure she was cloaking their movements."

"How did you get involved with them?"

"A contingent of the king's riders went missing, and he asked us to look into it. The slayers killed them." I decided not to tell her about being temporarily kicked out of the Citadel. "While investigating the bone flutes, I found the one responsible. He called himself the Carver."

"Where is he?"

"Dead."

"Good. Those things were a desecration of my kind."

We reached the main chamber where I'd first met the Assembly. The familiar long table was still there, but the chairs were all empty.

"Where is everyone?" I asked.

"They are on their way. I summoned them when I brought you inside."

Nemryth took a seat at the head of the table. I remained standing, impatient for her to hurry up and help Sion. Vandir the Great was the first to show, followed by Brold the Eternal. Tyrval the Cold arrived last. She smiled at me as she entered the room.

"As you all know, Risod is hunting the dragon slayers," Nemryth said. "Eldwin and Sion were attacked, and she has been poisoned. Tyrval, please see to her."

The old white-haired woman nodded and left. I wanted to go with her, but there was nothing I could do to help, so I stayed put.

"I'm sorry," Nemryth said, looking at me. "I thought we could take care of the threat before it affected anyone."

It surprised me to hear her apologize. Was this the same dragon that once took away my bond?

"I just want Sion to be all right."

"We fought many dragon slayers long ago, and we are not ill-prepared for their return. We have everything we need to combat them."

"Where did they come from?" I asked.

"They sailed across the ocean. We have not been able to determine what brought them here, but I suspect they ran out of dragons to kill in their own lands."

I wasn't sure what Nemryth was talking about. There was nothing across the ocean. At least, the maps I'd seen showed nothing beyond it. Given all the things I had seen, it wasn't hard for me to believe the maps were wrong. That might be where the Whispering Cliffs were.

"I've been having odd dreams lately about a place called the Whispering Cliffs. Does that name mean anything to you?"

Nemryth's head tilted slightly, and the corner of her lip twitched.

"Why would he dream of it?" Vandir asked lowly.

"Why indeed?" Nemryth cast a glance at the door Tyrval had left through. "What do you know of the cliffs?"

"Nothing," I replied. "That's why I asked."

"Before we knew we could bond with humans, all dragons lived in the wild. When you humans arrived, we could no longer live in peace. Men bring war and chaos wherever they go, and it was no different when they came to Osnen. At that time, we had not felt the cruelty of humanity. We trusted blindly and allowed humans to bond with our kind. It was then we saw humans wanted to weaponize us, to use us to their advantage."

This was the Nemryth I remembered. The memories must have brought back old pain, for she scowled.

"What does that have to do with the cliffs?"

"I'm getting to that," Nemryth snapped. "There were some dragons who refused to bond with humans. They left for another land and have not communicated with us since. I sent scouts out to find them just to ensure they were safe."

"Did they go to the Whispering Cliffs?"

"Some did. They wanted nothing to do with humanity, so I did not bother them. I'm sure there is a reason you are dreaming of the place, but I cannot fathom why."

I didn't know why I dreamed of the cliffs either, but at least I had some answers now. The Wild Ones were dragons. And not just any dragons, but untamed ones. I wonder if Anesko knew there were wild dragons out in the world. He had to, right? Yet if he did, why hadn't he sent anyone to find them?

"Where are the cliffs located?"

"I do not think it is prudent to tell you. Nothing good can come of it."

"You said yourself there is a reason I'm dreaming of the place. Perhaps to find out why I need to go there."

Before Nemryth could reply, Tyrval returned.

"How is she?" I asked. I could feel her presence in the bond, but she was still weak and didn't seem to be getting any better.

"The poison in her blood is powerful. It can be cured, but we don't have all the ingredients here in the temple."

"What are we lacking?" Nemryth asked.

"Whitedrop."

"What is that?" I asked.

"It's a flower that blooms in the shape of a teardrop," Tyrval replied. "It's white, hence its name, and it can only be found in the forest around the temple because we crafted it from magic."

"It should be easy to acquire, then."

"Not so much," Tyrval said. "When magic failed, it caused problems with the wards of the forest. We didn't notice anything at first, but as more time passed, we came to realize the magic had become warped, for lack of a better word."

"What does that mean?"

"The forest was designed to be a maze that prevented unwanted guests from finding us," Nemryth answered. "The magic still works, but it has strayed from its original purpose. We haven't explored it much since discovering this, but it may pose a problem in your search."

"My search?" I asked.

"You will need to find the flower," Tyrval said. "We will stay here and use our magic to hold off the poison from killing Sion, but it will take all our efforts. We will not be able to help you, else you risk losing your bonded."

"I'm not afraid to go alone."

I had been in the woods before. It had been a confusing experience, but there was nothing to be afraid of out there. At least, not then. It might be different now, but I'd faced more frightening things than a magical forest.

"Where can I find the flower?"

"When we created this place, we infused the first tree we planted with magic. We built all the wards upon it, and it is there you will find the whitedrop flower. The tree will not be easy to find, however. Part of its defense is illusion. It can use magic to confuse and disorient you, and the illusions it crafts will feel real."

I wished Maren was here with me, but I knew this was something I would have to do on my own. There was no sense in waiting around. Sion's life was in the balance.

"Where is the tree?" I asked. "And how will I know what tree I'm looking for?"

"The tree is north of here, and you'll know it when you see it."

That was vague and not very helpful, but I should have expected that kind of answer from the Assembly.

"Come," Nemryth said, looking at the other members. "We must hold off the poison until Eldwin can find the whitedrop."

6

The forest was strangely silent. No birds chirped in the trees above, and no animals skittered around in the thickets. I'd been to the temple twice before and had never encountered any sort of danger, but for some reason, this time felt different. There was an ominous feeling in the air that I couldn't shake.

I trudged through the brush with my hand resting on the hilt of my sword. Despite the lack of animal life, I thought I could see things moving in my peripherals. Each time I turned to look, there was nothing there.

The undergrowth abruptly cleared to reveal a path. It wound north and east, and I stepped onto it, glancing back the way I'd come. The top of the temple was still visible, but the dense foliage was close to blocking my view of it. Finding the tree was supposed to be the hard part, but what about returning to the temple? What if the magic didn't let me find my way back?

I decided not to dwell on that thought. It would only distract me from being vigilant. I followed the path north, rocks and other small debris crunching under my boots. My eyes continued to play tricks on me, and I knew it was the magic of the forest trying to keep me from my course. I would not be dissuaded, and I forged ahead.

The path turned softly to the right, but it was

still heading north, so I continued following it. I glanced back and saw the temple was out of sight now. The air was humid and heavy, and sweat was collecting on my forehead. I brushed it away with the back of my hand and stopped walking when I noticed the path was no longer heading in the right direction.

The path had barely turned, yet somehow, I was further east now. I didn't have time for this. Sion needed help, and this blasted forest was playing games with my patience. I drew my sword and pressed the tip against a nearby tree.

"I don't want to hurt you," I said aloud. "But I will. My dragon needs aid. If you don't show me the way to the tree, I will hack my way to it."

It was probably foolish to talk to the trees, given they weren't sentient, but my patience was gone. I pulled the sword away and turned back north, walking with purpose. I kept my blade ready in case I needed to prove a point to the magic. It seemed as though I blinked and I was right back at the same spot.

"This isn't real," I told myself. "It's an illusion."

That didn't make me feel any better. If anything, it infuriated me more. I raised my sword and swung it in a downward arc, chopping a sapling in half. It felt good to work my anger out, and I cut down another. And another. My anger fueled my swings, and I tore my blade through everything around me until I was panting heavily and my muscles burned so intensely I couldn't move my arm.

Underneath my anger was fear. The fear of losing Sion. She was a part of me as much as my own limbs. When our bond had briefly been severed on the Island of Lost Souls, I had never felt such pain. My connection to her was far different from what I had with Maren, and yet I felt as if losing Sion would devastate me far more than losing Maren. It was an odd realization.

And it spurred me into action. I sheathed my sword and looked around. I couldn't trust my eyes. They were being deceived by illusions. That left only my instincts, which weren't much use against magic, but it was better than nothing at all. Which way was truly north? I grabbed a sapling I'd cut and stabbed it vertically into the soil, marking the position of its shadow with a small stick. Then I waited.

A short while later, I marked the shadow's new location. The line between the two markings signified east to west, and now I knew which way was true north. I walked in that direction with my eyes closed to slits, not daring to believe what I saw was real. The forest shifted subtly around me, and the path curved to the right. Knowing it was merely the illusion at work, I continued straight ahead. A tall tree was in my way, and despite trusting my instincts, I flinched as I reached it.

I passed right through it, and the magic tingled against my flesh. It was akin to feeling a hair on you that you can't see. The forest shifted again, and once more I ignored the curving path. The ominous feeling I'd felt earlier gave way to something different, something more primal.

Panic.

Was the magic … afraid? No, that wasn't possible. At least, I didn't think so. It wasn't logical. And yet, I could feel it in the air around me. The scenery changed again, and this time, an enormous bear appeared. Its hair bristled as it saw me, and now I was no longer sure if it was only an illusion. The bear bellowed at me, the sound loud and harsh. I drew my sword and prepared myself to be mauled, but as the bear charged, it passed through me.

I exhaled a long breath, thankful it was only the magic. A wall of shrubbery blocked the way ahead, and I smiled. The illusions were less deceiving now. I sheathed my blade and ran ahead, only this time, there was no illusion. I crashed into real bushes, and these had thorns. They sliced open my skin wherever they touched, but the pain was only a minor annoyance. I pushed my way through the wall, branches creaking and snapping.

And then I was through. I rubbed at the cuts on my arms to assuage the irritation and froze. A massive tree with countless limbs towered high into the air in front of me. The surrounding trees were like nothing more than seedlings in comparison. A thick white blanket around its base spread outward, and I realized it was an ocean of flowers.

Whitedrop. I'd found it! I rushed forward and knelt outside the flowers, not wanting to trample them. Neither Nemryth nor Tyrval told me how much they needed, so I plucked a dozen and stuffed them into the pouch at my side. I hesitated, not wanting to come back here again. A few more wouldn't hurt. I added some more to my collection and stood. The tree was old, older than any I had ever seen before. Its limbs stretched so far up that they cast an enormous shadow over the clearing.

The tree exuded power. With little thought about what I was doing, I bowed my head in its direction.

"Thank you," I whispered.

And then I turned and left, sprinting through the woods back to the temple.

7

Getting back was far easier than reaching the tree, but I knew it was because there was no magic trying to thwart me. Tyrval and the others were standing near Sion, their eyes closed and their hands outstretched toward her. I gently laid a hand on Tyrval's shoulder. Her eyes fluttered open.

"Did you find it?" she asked softly.

I nodded.

She lowered her left hand and extended her right. I withdrew the whitedrop from my pouch and placed it in her palm.

"Is that enough?"

"More than enough," Tyrval replied. "One flower is potent enough to cure a dozen dragons from this poison."

"So Sion will be all right?"

"That remains to be seen, but I am confident in my abilities. I know you have many questions about your dreams, but they will have to wait until I am done."

"How do you know about my dreams?" I asked.

"Who do you think gave them to you, my boy?"

"Wait, it was you? Why?"

"Sion first," she reminded.

"Yes, of course."

Tyrval went to work preparing a potion using the whitedrop while the other Assembly members continued working their magic. I felt useless, so I knelt beside Sion and laid my head against her neck, diving into the bond. I offered all the comfort I could manage, pushing it through to her end. She was weaker than before, but she responded by brushing my mind with hers.

I'm sorry, she whispered.

For what?

Allowing myself to be poisoned.

It wasn't your fault, I replied. *We didn't know what we were up against. Tyrval is mixing something for you now that should heal you.*

Where are we?

At the Temple of the Bond. I didn't want to come here, but it was the only option. The Citadel didn't have a cure for you.

How did we get here? I remember reaching the farm, and then ... there's nothing after that.

Master Katori sent us here with her magic.

A flash of pain flooded the bond, and I winced.

The poison is worsening, Sion said.

I opened my eyes and turned to look for Tyrval. She was coming out of the temple, a vial in her hands. She joined me and gently laid a hand on her Sion's snout.

"That's all you made?" I asked, thinking the vial was too small.

"This may be too much," she replied. "A few drops should do the trick. I'll need your help to open her jaws. Whitedrop works best under the tongue."

Relief is coming, I told Sion. *Don't bite me.*

You don't have to worry about that, she sighed. *I can't move.*

I got to my feet and planted them firmly, grabbed onto Sion's upper jaw, and heaved with all my might. Her teeth parted and Tyrval quickly reached into her mouth and placed a few drops under Sion's tongue, then snatched her hand back. I lowered Sion's jaw and wiped the saliva that got on my hands onto my pants.

"How long will it take to work?" I asked.

"It'll reach her bloodstream within a few moments, but it will take a few hours to eliminate the poison from her body completely. She will not be able to fly for a full day, maybe two."

We didn't have anywhere we needed to be, so that wasn't a problem. I would need to send word to Anesko somehow so that he knew everything was fine.

"Walk with me," Tyrval bade.

"I don't think I should leave her," I replied, looking at Sion. The cure might be in her body now, but until she was healed, we weren't safe yet.

"We will watch over her," Nemryth said.

I hesitated, but Tyrval took my hand in hers and pulled me away. I didn't fight her but fell into step beside her.

"Our history is long and complicated, as I'm sure you've gleaned from Nemryth."

"She told me about the Wild Ones if that's what you mean."

"Yes, that is what I'm talking about."

"Why have you been making me dream of them?"

"Surely you know," Tyrval chuckled, glancing at me as we walked along the edge of the temple grounds.

"No? I've been confused since the time they started."

"The Order is crumbling. There are too many problems and not enough riders to deal with them. Since there are no dragons to be found, there can be no new riders. Quite a conundrum, yes?"

"That's why I've been tracking those who trade them illegally."

"That will take too much time. And if you managed to track them all down, their numbers still wouldn't be enough."

"How do you know?"

"That is a secret I will not reveal. It doesn't matter anyway, my boy, so don't try prying. Stay focused. You need dragons. Lots of them. You can find them at the Whispering Cliffs."

"Nemryth said they are untamed and want nothing to do with humans," I said.

"That was long ago," Tyrval replied, shrugging. "We may be stubborn, but even a dragon's mind can be changed with time. I sent you the dreams to pique your interest in searching for them. The Wild Ones are the only answer to the dilemma the Order faces."

"Why would you help us? I thought you regretted making the deal with humans?"

"*I* regret nothing. Nemryth said that, and I doubt she truly feels that way. Even if she did, I'm sure she's changed her stance. Dragons and humans cannot survive without one another."

"What do you mean?" I asked.

"Do not worry about that right now. There are enough problems to deal with today. Leave tomorrow's where they are."

Her words sounded forbidding. Was that a warning of something, or merely a fact? Had the pact dragons made with humans sealed their fate, or was it something worse? I pushed the thought away. As Tyrval said, we had enough problems right now.

"You gave me the dreams to make me seek out the wild dragons, but how would I do that? I don't know where the Whispering Cliffs are."

"I thought you would figure it out on your own,

but it seems I will have to give you the answer. You will need to cross the end of the world and continue beyond the horizon."

I repeated the words in my mind, trying to make sense of them, but it was futile. I stopped walking and stared at her. She continued ahead a few steps before turning around.

"What is it?" she asked.

"You always speak in riddles or with vague notions, and I have no patience for that. Where are the cliffs?"

Tyrval's aged lips curled up into a smile, the wrinkles smoothing out.

"You are lucky I like you," she said. "I do not freely give wisdom to anyone else. On your maps, what lies to the west?"

I scrunched my brow, trying to visualize a map in my mind. "Valgaard."

"Beyond that."

"I'm not sure. I haven't been past Valgaard."

"If you continue onward, you will find an ocean. Many believe there is nothing on the other side of the water, but that is not true. The Whispering Cliffs are there, as well as many other things, all of them dangerous. You must brave these perils to go where the dragons reside."

8

I stared at Tyrval for a long moment in silence.

"Can't you get them to return?"

"No."

"Why not?"

"You must convince them to bond with humans," she replied. "You are a human, and they will see your true character. If they like what they see, they may be swayed to come."

"What if they kill me?"

"Then at least you tried, my boy." Tyrval smiled.

"That's so comforting," I said sarcastically.

"The Order will fall if there are no more dragons to bond with. Do you think that is an acceptable risk?"

I had asked myself that question many times. It weighed on me constantly, following me like a dark cloud. Everyone, including Anesko, was doing what they could to ensure the Order would continue, yet there didn't seem to be any progress. If anything, we continued to lose riders.

"I think the benefit outweighs the risk, but why me? Master Anesko could go, or Master Katori. They have authority and the experience needed for something this important."

"You saved Osnen. Twice, I might add. I think you are more capable than you give yourself credit for."

"I didn't do it alone," I replied. "And one of those times it was my fault the world was in jeopardy. If I fail …" The words brought back the image of T'Mere lying in a pool of blood.

"You must not fear failure," Tyrval said. "It is an agent of learning. If you don't fail, you don't learn. And if you don't learn, you don't change."

She was right. I often learned something valuable from making a mistake, but this seemed too big to risk messing up. And yet, she was determined for me to go.

"I'll consider it," I said. "Sion is my sole concern right now."

"She will recover soon."

"Nemryth said the dragon slayers came from across the ocean," I changed the subject. "Is that the same place as the cliffs?"

"No. The cliffs are in the west. The dragon slayers came from the lands south of here."

South? The world was bigger than I imagined. When I was on the Island of Lost Souls, I'd seen the spirits of races called elves and dwarves. Perhaps those lands were where the slayers had come from. It had been dark when they attacked, but I was fairly certain they were human. Hopefully, Risod would find them before they killed any more dragons.

"You said it would be a day or two before Sion can fly. What do I do until then?"

"Whatever you want," Tyrval said. "You aren't a prisoner here."

She patted me on the shoulder and returned to the front of the temple. While I knew the Assembly wouldn't keep me from going anywhere, that didn't mean the forest wouldn't. Not that I wanted to leave Sion or anything, but some time to myself to clear my mind might be a good idea.

I wandered around the immediate grounds of the temple, careful not to stray into the boundary of the forest. My heart was troubled, and not just for Sion. I missed Maren dearly. The Order was on the brink of falling apart, and dragon slayers were roaming the land. There were so many problems, and I felt as though I didn't have the strength to face them all. I was tired.

No, I was weary. I continuously forged ahead because I had to, because others relied on me. Or was that merely an excuse? Perhaps Tyrval was right, that I was stronger than I gave myself credit for. And yet, despite my strength, I was always making mistakes. The people of Osnen viewed my father as a hero. Had he ever made major mistakes as I had? Probably not, though I would never know that for sure. My father had saved Osnen from the False King.

And you did the same thing, my inner voice reminded.

That was mostly true. It seemed so long ago

now. I inhaled a deep breath and slowly released it, pushing away all the thoughts that plagued me. As Tyrval said, today had enough of its own problems to contend with. I returned to where Sion lay and sat down, leaning my back against her. The warmth of her body heat comforted me as few things could, and I closed my eyes to rest them for a moment.

The next thing I knew, I was huddled among a group of young dragons. They were all different colors, and they were cowered in fear. I was afraid, too. A man stood in front of me, tall and dark. He held an instrument in his hand that caused great pain, but I wasn't sure how I knew that.

"Come here, beast," the man said. His voice was baritone, his words threatening. One of the dragons slunk forward, its tail curled up close to its body. Why were we all afraid of this man? We outnumbered him and could tear him limb from limb. Wait, why did I envision latching my jaws on his head and crunching hard?

The man swung the instrument at the slinking dragon, and the air buzzed with magic as it struck the dragon across the side of the face. I flinched and looked down at my claws, digging them deep into the sand and clenching them tightly. Wait, I had claws.

I jolted and snapped my eyes open. Panicked, I looked down at my hands. There were no claws, only my normal human hands. Sion growled in her sleep, and I realized it wasn't my dream, but hers. No, not a dream. A nightmare. It was one of the traumatic memories of her past when she was a captive to those blasted dragon traders who'd tortured her before I'd found her.

"It's all right," I whispered, running a hand along the scales of her neck. She stopped growling, but she continued to stir in her sleep. I looked around and realized it was dark. A thin drab blanket was draped across my lower body, and I saw Nemryth sitting cross-legged a few feet away. She was facing the woods.

I rolled the blanket up and set it aside, then stood and walked over to her. She looked up at me and nodded at the ground beside her. I sat down, stretching my legs out in front of me.

"What are you doing out here?" I asked softly, not wanting to wake Sion.

"Contemplating," she replied. "The night helps me."

Her words surprised me, though I suppose they shouldn't have. She was a black dragon, after all.

"What are you thinking about?"

"Many things."

"Such as?"

"Why must you humans feel the need to know everything?"

I shrugged. "Probably because our lives are so brief."

Nemryth snorted, but I could see the hint of a smile in her hard expression.

"I'm thinking about the dragon slayers."

"It is curious that they are here," I said. "Tyrval said they came from a land to the south."

"Yes. They sailed here from a place far beyond the Island of Lost Souls. It is a miracle they made it here at all. Those waters are treacherous."

"Do you think they intended to come here?"

"I suppose it is possible their arrival was an accident, but if Osnen wasn't their destination, why are they still here?"

"I think the answer to that question is rather simple. Osnen is a good place to be to hunt dragons, whether arriving on accident or not. They must have sensed the presence of dragons and decided to stay. Has Risod found them yet?"

"Not since the last time I heard from her. She should have reported in by now, so maybe she's taking care of them."

"I pray that's the case," I said.

"Save your prayers. The gods don't listen to us."

I looked at Nemryth in my peripheral. Her tone didn't sound bitter, but the words themselves did. Her expression hadn't changed. An indifferent statement, then?

"What if the slayers captured her? Or worse?" I didn't want to ask the question, but I knew we were both thinking about it.

Nemryth's eyes hardened. "Then the Assembly will go to war."

9

The next morning, I awoke to find Sion was gone.

I sat up and looked around, my heart racing wildly.

I'm fine, she said, sensing my panic. *I was thirsty.*

I laid back down and stared up at the sky. That she was up and moving of her own accord was a good sign. My neck was stiff, and I rolled onto my side to ease the strain. I didn't remember falling asleep. The last thing I recalled was lying down beside Sion and staring at the stars.

How are you feeling? I asked.

Better. I don't feel any of the poison in my blood.

That's good. Tyrval had a cure. I just had to get one of the ingredients. I projected the memories of the day before to her. The bond filled with her amusement.

The wards are … damaged, she said.

Yes. Nemryth said the forest has been acting strangely ever since magic failed. It seems restoring the flow did not fix the wards.

Did you warn Master Anesko of the dragon slayers?

I did. Master Katori tried to help you, but the poison was beyond her abilities. She got us here using her magic. Risod has been trying to track the slayers down, but no luck yet.

I'm famished, Sion said. *I'm going to find breakfast.*

Don't stray too far. If something happens to you ...

I'll be fine. If I need help, I will let you know.

The sound of cracking branching signaled Sion's departure further into the woods. I rose to my feet and brushed myself off, then entered the temple. I hoped the Assembly had food. My stomach rumbled, and I knew if I didn't eat soon, I wouldn't have the energy to do much. I headed for the main room and saw Tyrval seated at the table. A loaf of bread and a plate covered with cheese and various fruits were in front of her, untouched. She looked up at me as I sat across from her.

"You going to eat that?" I asked with a smile.

Tyrval mirrored my expression and pushed the plate toward me. There was something about her smile that seemed forced.

"Is everything all right?"

"I'm not sure. Nemryth is worried about Risod."

"She never checked in last night?"

Tyrval shook her head.

I grabbed an apple off the plate and took a bite. I chewed in silence, a myriad of terrible scenarios running through my mind.

"Nemryth said there would be war if something happened."

"She wasn't exaggerating. She'll burn everything in her path to find Risod."

"I don't blame her, though I hope she doesn't do that. Innocent people would be caught in the middle." I took another bite of the apple and stared at Tyrval. "What's the plan?"

"There isn't one yet. We don't want to fly into a trap."

A humming noise filled the room, and I creased my brow in confusion. Tyrval touched the surface of the table and it rippled like water. A face appeared. Maren's face.

"Maren?"

"Eldwin? Can you hear me?"

"Y-yes," I stuttered in surprise.

"Master Anesko asked me to try and reach you. How's Sion?"

"She's fine. Tyrval administered a cure for the poison."

"That's great news. What about you? I heard you found the one making the dragon bone flutes."

"I was worried about Sion, but I'm all right now. I miss you."

"I miss you, too. Master Anesko wants you to return to the Citadel as soon as possible."

"What's wrong?" I asked.

"Nothing. With dragon slayers prowling Osnen, he wants all riders and their dragons at the school for their safety."

"I'll return as soon as I can. Sion is recovering. Until she's regained her strength, I don't want to press her too much."

"Be careful when you come back," Maren said. "Those crazy people could be anywhere."

"I will. You will see me soon. I promise."

"I love you, Eldwin."

"I love you more."

Maren rolled her eyes playfully and waved. The image on the table faded, and the surface returned to wood.

"Do you think the slayers are powerful enough to capture or kill Risod?" I asked.

"I want to say no, but I know better than that. We lost many of our kind to their hands long ago. We dragons thrive on magic, but it is also our weakness. You can hit us with swords and arrows all day and they will do nothing but enchant the weapons and they can pierce our scales and end our lives. That these ones wield magic makes them very dangerous."

I wanted to offer to search for Risod, but I had enough on my plate to deal with already. That, and I didn't really want to face those slayers again without a small army. I tore a piece from the bread and popped it into my mouth. It was freshly baked and had a nice buttery flavor.

"If you'll excuse me, I need to speak with Nemryth," Tyrval said, rising from her chair.

I nodded as my mouth was full, and she left. It was quiet, too quiet for my liking. I finished the rest of the food and went back outside. Sion had returned and was pacing back and forth in front of the temple.

What are you doing? I asked.

There's something about this place that bothers me. We should go.

What do you mean? The temple is probably the safest place outside of the Citadel.

I didn't say it was dangerous, Sion replied. *I said it bothers me. The distortion of the magic makes me uncomfortable. Can we leave?*

I glanced around at the trees. There was nothing out of the ordinary to me, but I wasn't magically inclined.

You haven't had much time to rest, I said. *I don't want you to hurt yourself by flying.*

I am strong, she argued. *I can fly.*

I had a feeling it wasn't a good idea, but I wanted to get back to the Citadel.

Promise me that if you start feeling weak, you'll land and rest. I know it's dangerous with the slayers on the prowl, but we can't risk you falling from the sky.

You have my word.

I looked back at the temple. With Risod missing, they probably didn't need the added hassle of Sion and me being here.

Fine. Give me a minute.

I wandered out of sight and relieved myself, then returned and climbed up Sion's shoulder and seated myself in the saddle.

Take us home, I said.

Sion launched into the air and turned west. I just hoped we didn't run into the slayers.

10

We left the temple behind and traveled a few miles before Sion began struggling.

Land, I told her.

She didn't argue, which told me that even her stubbornness couldn't combat how she was feeling. She landed on the flat portion of a rocky hill. Her sides flexed continuously with her panting, and I slid out of the saddle and stood beside her while she rested, my sword drawn. I watched the landscape around us intently.

Be at ease, Sion said. *I do not sense anyone nearby.*

Are you all right? I asked her, not putting my guard down.

Yes. I just need some rest. The poison was more taxing than I realized.

I told her I didn't think she was ready to fly yet, but there was no arguing with a dragon.

No, there isn't, Sion said, her mirth filling the bond.

Yeah, yeah, I replied. *I can't wait to be home. I miss Maren.*

As do I.

My conversation with Tyrval was in the back of my mind, but I had yet to decide on whether I was going to find the wild dragons or not. I leaned up against Sion and sent the memory through the bond.

What do you think?

I think it sounds like an adventure. I love adventures.

Do you think the wild dragons will agree to bond with humans, though?

You are an excellent human. It was because of you we rescued the dragons held captive in Ilok. Those dragons willingly came to the Citadel.

They came because they trusted you, not me.

They trusted me more, but that does not mean they didn't trust you at all. They would not have come despite my words had they doubted your intentions.

I suppose that's true. I'll need to convince Anesko to let us go. He wants every rider at the school until the slayers are dealt with.

Has he reinstated you at the school?

Not yet, I replied.

Then you do not answer to him. If you want to go, we will go.

I smiled and shook my head. Sion sounded a lot like Maren sometimes. Perhaps I was drawn to those who broke the rules for a reason, though I couldn't guess what that reason was.

No, I need to do right by Anesko. We will go to the Citadel.

Very well.

Sion rested for half an hour while I kept a close watch on our surroundings. There was nothing of concern, but I refused to get comfortable. That's when I made mistakes. When she felt strong enough to fly again, I mounted up and we continued west. We were close to Istral, the seat of the throne of Osnen, when it occurred to me that the king was looking for me.

We should probably go around Istral so we don't have any trouble, I told Sion.

Too late, she replied. *Looks like we've got company.*

I leaned to the right and glanced down. A contingent of the king's riders was quickly winging their way up toward us.

I can't outrun them. I'm too tired.

I know.

Deep down, I'd been hoping she would bolt ahead, but I knew that was foolish. She was doing all she could just to stay in the air. Fleeing wasn't an option. While I was curious to know what Erling wanted with me, I wanted the meeting to be on my terms. It looked like that wasn't an option now. They quickly surrounded us, and the captain in charge met my gaze. Sion flapped her wings to keep herself steady in place, but she was exhausting her remaining energy. Maybe I could make this quick.

The captain wore the same armor as the others of his group, but he had an emblem of a shield with two swords crossed over it emblazoned on his pauldron, signifying his rank. An ugly scar ran the length of the left side of his face, narrowly missing his eye.

"Hail, rider," he said. "The skies are off limits. What are you doing out here?"

They don't know who I am, I told Sion. *Maybe this will go better than I thought.*

Maybe.

"Good day, captain. I wasn't aware the skies were off-limits. I'm returning to the Citadel at the behest of Master Anesko. He's recalled us all back to the school."

"A wise move by the master," the captain said. "There's a murderer on the loose, a former rider of the school."

His words had me reeling. I ran through the members of the school in my mind, but I couldn't figure out who he was talking about.

"A murderer?"

"Yes. His name is Eldwin Baines. He was banished from the school, and then he killed a rider and a dragon."

Realization dawned on me. Rouzet and his dragon. Erling was blaming me for their deaths? But of course he was. Even if he knew the truth, he would use it to his advantage simply because he didn't like me. I cleared my throat.

"That's terrible news indeed. I wasn't aware of

that.”

“You’re lucky we found you before he did, then. Have you been to Istral before?”

I nodded.

“Excellent. We’ll escort you to the stable. You’ll have to stay in the city until we find the traitor.”

“I’ll be fine,” I assured him. “Master Anesko will be worried about me if I don’t return, so I really need to get back.”

“You can send him a message letting him know you’re safe. We cannot let you go any further.”

I knew defeat when I saw it, so I nodded.

“Lead the way, captain.”

The riders escorted us down, all the way to the stable. I hesitantly dismounted and glanced around. I doubted any of the guards would recognize me, but it was likely someone might remember my face. One rider landed a few feet away, and the others wheeled overhead a few times before leaving. The rider who landed jumped down from the saddle and nodded at me as he strode past.

We need to lie low until we have the opportunity get away while no one is watching, I said.

I needed the break anyway, Sion replied. *We’re safer in the city with enemies we know than out there.*

She had a point. I rubbed her snout with my palm and stared at her. The weariness was evident in her eyes.

I'm sorry, I said. *I should have made you stay at the temple for another day or two.*

Do not apologize, she huffed. *It was I who wanted to leave. I do not regret my decision, and neither should you. We will return to the Citadel soon. Be patient.*

I am impatient, I admitted, *but that's not my concern. I worry about your health, but also what Erling has in mind for me. It can't be good.*

I will burn the castle to ash if he touches you.

"Sure you will," I said aloud, smiling.

"Over there," someone said.

I turned to look. It was the rider. He was pointing at me. Standing next to him was Erling.

"Eldwin." The king's tone was surprisingly friendly, but the way he looked at me said his feelings were quite the opposite. He motioned to the soldier.

"Escort him to my chambers."

11

Sion growled threateningly.

It's all right, I said. *But be ready to make a run for it.*

I won't leave you behind, Sion replied.

Good. I projected a memory to her from my first meeting with the king when he cornered me on a balcony. *When I give you the word, find me there.*

I will.

"Your Majesty," I greeted Erling, sweeping into a bow.

The soldier strode up and grabbed me harshly by my left arm.

"There's no need for that," I said. "I'll go willingly."

The soldier looked at Erling, who nodded, and he released me. Erling turned around and headed back into the palace, and the soldier stayed at my side as I followed the king. Nothing about the palace was familiar to me, but it had been a while since I'd been here. That, and the first and only visit I'd made had been during less than ideal circumstances.

We walked along an enormous hall, past the throne room, and into a lavish chamber. A few servants were busy cleaning.

"Leave us," Erlin demanded.

The servants scattered and fled the room, and the soldier shut the door, taking up a stance in front of it. I found it curious that he hadn't taken my sword, but the king probably wasn't concerned about me trying to do anything. And he was right. If things went ill, I planned to flee. Erling walked over to a tall window and stared out at the city, his hands clasped behind his back.

"Have you come to return my money?" he asked.

"No, Your Majesty, but I will pay you back."

"What of my captain, Rouzet. Did you kill him?"

"No."

Erling turned from the window and looked at me.

"I sent him to arrest you. He sent a message that you were in his custody, and then suddenly he's dead and you were nowhere to be found. Tell me then, how do you explain his death?"

"We were attacked," I said. "By the same people who killed your riders near Ilok. They are dragon slayers."

"Dragon slayers? Do you think I am a fool?"

"Not at all, Your Majesty. You are as wise as an owl and as crafty as a serpent."

"Flattery will get you nowhere, Eldwin. Your crimes against the kingdom are great, and they continue to stack upon one another."

"I have not committed any crimes," I retorted. "If anything, I've sacrificed more than you to save this kingdom from destruction."

Erling laughed.

"You would make a good jester if I had need of one." His smile faded, and his expression turned into a scowl. "Listen carefully, you worthless lowborn. I want the truth from you, or I'll lock you in the dungeon and kill your dragon. Did Anesko assassinate my riders?"

I scrunched my face. "What? No. He would never do something like that. Dragon slayers killed them. If you don't believe me, send one of your sorcerers to check. I'm sure they can conjure up the past and see it for themselves."

"Let's say it was dragon slayers. Who hired them?"

"No one. At least, I don't think so. I've been trying to find out where they came from, and so far, it seems they sailed across the ocean to get here."

Erling snorted. "There's nothing across the water. If there was, I'd know. If you won't admit that your master orchestrated the attack on my riders, then I will be forced to brand you as a traitor. Do you know what happens to traitors?"

I shook my head. This wasn't exactly what I was expecting, but it didn't really surprise me, either. The political strife between the Order and the king was no secret, but what was Erling going to gain by framing Anesko for something he didn't do?

"I hang them on the gallows."

"Why do you think Anesko would do something so stupid?" I asked, genuinely curious.

"Do you truly think he is happy with his lot in life? He's a babysitter. I know he desires more. Tell me what I want and I will forgive all of your crimes. I'll even expand the lands I gave to your father and make you a lord over my nobles. How does the title of baron sound?"

He's trying to bribe you, Sion said.

Yes, but why?

What is the one thing the king doesn't control?

I considered the question, and the answer dawned on me. Why hadn't I seen it before?

The Order. He wants the riders to answer to him.

"I don't enjoy repeating myself," Erling said.

"Anesko had nothing to do with it. You're trying to make an accusation that has no base in the truth."

"You disappoint me, Eldwin. I thought you would make the right decision." He looked past me to the soldier at the door. "Lock him in the dungeon. Maybe some time alone will convince him to change his mind."

Get ready, I told Sion. *We're going to need to*

make a hasty departure. Once we get some distance between us and Istral, we'll land and hide somewhere.

I'll get us to the Citadel, Sion replied.

No. I don't want you risking your life. We'll take refuge somewhere.

Sion didn't argue, but I could feel her rebellious attitude in the bond. She wasn't going to listen to me. The soldier drew his sword and pointed the tip at me.

"Disarm yourself," he said.

Several thoughts ran through my mind. The first was that I was probably going to die. Second, how I didn't want to die yet. Third, I glanced around the room and eyed the window. The glass looked too thick to break on my own, and Sion didn't know where I was. *I* didn't even know where I was.

Keep to the plan. I see the place you showed me in your memory, Sion said.

The balcony. I needed to get to the balcony. I reached down and pretended to be undoing my belt, then quickly unsheathed my blade and rushed the soldier. Our swords met with a clang, and I used all my strength to push his arm wide, then drove my shoulder into his chest, slamming him against the wall. I yanked the door open and fled into the hallway, frantically looking for my way of escape. I got halfway down the hall before I heard a bell clang.

Hurry, Sion urged. *There are many soldiers*

running to the castle.

I ran faster, and a wave of relief washed over me. At the end of the hall, the palace was open to the outside. The familiar wide, circular balcony came into view.

I'm almost there.

I reached the balcony and skidded to a stop, looking behind me. A dozen or more guards were coming for me. I climbed atop the stone railing and peered down. My stomach churned at the thought of falling, and I found it odd I never experienced that fear while flying. I looked for Sion, but I didn't see her.

Where are you?

I'm coming, she huffed.

Her sleek red body came rushing up from the city below. I could hear the clamor of the guards behind me. It was now or never. I sheathed my blade and leaped off the railing. A scream escaped me despite my best effort to hold it in. The wind rushed past my ears, and I landed hard on Sion's back. I scurried along her scales to the saddle and sat down. Looking back, I saw the guards on the balcony. And standing among them was Erling, his face red with anger.

Find somewhere to hide. We won't be able to outdistance them.

Don't tell me what to do, Sion growled. She headed west for the Citadel.

12

Sion flew as long as she could, but we were still a few miles from the school when her breathing became labored more than normal. I continuously looked back, and though I didn't see anyone in pursuit, I doubted Erling would allow me to escape without repercussion.

Find somewhere to land, I said.

No.

I don't want you to hurt yourself.

I'm fine.

She clearly wasn't fine, considering how much she was struggling. I was worried she was going to push herself too hard and something disastrous was going to happen. If she wouldn't heed my words, then I would give her as much of my own strength as I could. Learning from the last time, I leaned down close to her and closed my eyes, then sent some of my energy flowing into the bond.

I thought she was going to protest, but she didn't. She allowed me to help her, but I wasn't sure how much good it did. She was still struggling, and I knew if I didn't limit what I gave her, it could very likely kill me.

No more, Sion said. *I will make it to the school.*

I cut off the flow and sat back up. My vision blurred for a moment as I got lightheaded, but it faded quickly. I looked back, and this time, I saw a contingent of the king's riders.

We've got company.

I turned my gaze ahead. The school was visible now, though we still had some distance to go before we arrived. The king's riders were fairly far back, but they would catch up to us soon. It was going to be close.

We'll get there before they catch us, Sion vowed.

Despite her exhaustion, she picked up the pace. I ground my teeth anxiously, praying she was right, but also praying she didn't injure herself.

As soon as we're within range for you to speak with Demris, tell him to alert Master Anesko.

We sped over the landscape, but every time I glanced back, the king's riders had closed the distance a little more. The farm where I'd left Sion to get help passed beneath us, and I held out hope we might actually make it to safety. A few minutes later, I could make out the guards atop the walls of the Citadel.

A roar split the air behind us, but I didn't look. I kept my focus ahead as if that would somehow help. We crossed over the wall and a magical barrier erupted from the ground, reaching up to shield the school within a protective dome. Now I did look back, just in time to see one of the king's dragons slam into the barrier. It roared in anger and pain, but it didn't appear to be seriously harmed.

Sion landed roughly in the courtyard near the stable, and I saw Master Anesko and Master Katori, as well as Maren, come rushing out of the school.

"What's going on?" Maren asked.

I climbed out of the saddle and leaped down to the ground, patting Sion's neck comfortingly.

Go get some rest, I told her.

She nuzzled me in the chest and slowly made her way below ground. Maren wrapped her arms around me, and I held onto her tightly for a long moment.

"Your father wants to take over the Order," I finally said.

She pulled back, her face contorted in a look of confusion. "My father? Where did you hear that?"

"From him," I replied. "Not in so many words, but his intent was obvious. He wanted me to say that Anesko was behind the death of his riders."

"That's insane," she said.

I looked past her to Anesko as he strode over to us.

"How is Sion?" he asked.

"She's fine. Well, she will be. The Assembly had a cure for the poison, but she's still recovering. A few days of rest and she should be back to normal."

"That's good news." He looked to where the king's riders were. "What's that about?"

"Erling claims you are behind the murder of his riders. I don't know that he actually believes that. I think he's using an opportunity to try and take more power for himself. He wanted me to say you were guilty so he could remove you from the school and take over."

"He said that? All of it?"

"Pretty much," I replied. "I escaped the palace, but he sent them after me."

"Don't worry about them," Anesko replied. "We will not let them in, nor will we surrender you to the king."

"My father always gets his way," Maren said. "He will not be happy about being thwarted."

"Let me worry about the king. His actions are not entirely unexpected, but I didn't think he would be so bold in his quest to rule over the Order."

"Master," a breathless guard called out. "The royal riders request your presence."

Anesko nodded and headed for the eastern wall. Maren and I exchanged glances and followed him. We climbed the stone stairs that led to the ramparts, and one of the king's riders, the captain who had stopped me, landed his dragon near the wall. He climbed up his dragon's neck to stand atop her head.

"Master Anesko?" he asked.

"I am."

"Good. You shall deliver Eldwin Baines over to

me immediately, by order of the king."

"What are his charges?" Anesko asked.

"He is a traitor to Osnen and a murderer."

"Eldwin is many things, but he is neither of those. Do you have proof of these crimes?"

"No," the captain answered, some of his bluster gone. "But the king's word is above contestation."

"That sounds like something a tyrant would say, don't you think?"

The captain frowned.

"I implore you to hand him over. The king will not be pleased if I return without him."

"That is your problem, not mine. My loyalty is to this school and its members first. The king falls much lower on my list."

The captain sputtered angrily. "How dare you! The king can have this school torn apart, brick by brick, if he chooses. You will hand over the criminal now, or I will tell the king that you are also a traitor, that this entire school is full of traitors."

Master Katori joined us on the wall, moving to stand beside Anesko. She stared at the captain in silence for a moment, then looked over her shoulder at the men guarding the walls.

"I see no traitors here except you and your men," she said. "We will not turn Eldwin over to you. Begone from here."

The captain looked at Anesko. "Does this

woman speak for you?"

"Master Katori does not speak *for* me, but *with* me. My answer is no, captain. Tell your king whatever you like, but Eldwin is staying here."

"Fools, the lot of you!" The captain spat to the side and returned to his saddle, urging his dragon into the air. He rejoined his men, and the entire contingent turned and left.

"Thank you, Master," I said softly.

"Don't thank me yet. I may have just doomed us all."

<h1 style="text-align:center">13</h1>

I sat in the dining hall, staring off at the wall while my food got cold. Maren was sitting across from me, and I could feel her eyes on me. I blinked a few times and returned her stare.

"What?"

"You tell me," she replied. "You daydreaming?"

"Sort of. Sorry. I … the last week has been a lot."

"What happened while you were gone?"

I glanced around the hall. There were a few people at the other tables, and I lowered my voice.

"Promise you won't say anything to Anesko."

"You know I won't say anything if you ask me not to."

"I found out who was making the bone flutes."

"You did? How?"

"Luck, mostly. Anesko told me not to look into it while I was suspended, but I did anyway."

"You were supposed to be learning from your mistakes," Maren said.

"I know, but this was important. Everyone has been too busy to look into it, and since I technically was no longer part of the school, I figured, why not?" I shrugged.

"What did you find out?"

"He called himself the Carver."

"Called?"

"Yeah. He's dead now."

"You killed him?"

"Sion did, but I allowed her to. Encouraged it, even." Replaying the memory, I almost felt guilty about it. Almost. "He didn't deserve to live."

"I remember a time when you didn't think it was your place to decide who lived and who died," Maren said darkly.

"That was different," I replied, growing defensive. "The Carver was evil. Evil doesn't count."

"I'm not judging you, Eldwin. I'm just stating a fact."

"I also learned something from the Assembly. The dragon slayers are from another land."

"What does that mean?"

"They sailed here from across the ocean. Nemryth thinks they arrived here by mistake, but stayed because there were dragons for them to kill. There's something else, too. Remember my nightmares?"

Maren nodded.

"Tyrval was sending them to me."

"Why?"

"She said something cryptic about the survival of humans and dragons, but she wouldn't explain what she meant. Anyway, there are wild dragons at the Whispering Cliffs. Tyrval wants me to go there and convince the dragons to come here."

"Wild dragons? There haven't been any wild dragons in Osnen since … well, it's always been this way that I know of."

"That's what I thought, too. Apparently, there were some who didn't agree with the deal the Assembly made to allow humans to bond with them. They left Osnen for a land in the west."

"Valgaard?"

"No. It's beyond the ocean."

I could see the wheels turning behind Maren's eyes.

"Have you told Anesko?"

"Not yet. I still haven't decided if I want to go."

"What are you talking about? This is what we've been looking for. More dragons. The Order will die out without them."

"Trust me, I've been telling myself that for a while now, but I need Anesko's blessing. My word means nothing to him, whether he knows it or not. I want to earn this from him instead of sneaking off. Especially since we don't know what's going to happen with your father."

"I admire your ability to see your flaws," Maren said. "I admire a lot about you, but it's all the small things that made me fall in love with you."

"You mean it wasn't my fortune?" I joked.

She rolled her eyes. "It was lonely here without you. I'm glad you're home."

"I felt the same way out there. I'm sure Sion was tired of feeling my sadness."

We locked eyes and stared at one another in silence for a while. Finally, Maren stood and picked up her tray.

"Let's talk to Anesko about these wild dragons. We'll need them more than ever now."

"What do you mean?" I asked.

"My father's rage knows no bounds. I doubt he's changed since I left, which means he's likely mobilizing his army to march on the Citadel."

Erling was crazy, but would he really go to war with the Order? Nothing good could come of it, but who would stop him? We were vastly outnumbered. Unless we had more dragons on our side. Maren was always one step ahead of me, and I loved her all the more for it.

I hurriedly shoveled the cold ham on my plate into my mouth, wolfing it down, then stood up. We returned our trays and left the dining hall, making our way to Anesko's office. Master Katori was with him, and they stopped talking when Maren and I walked in.

"We're a bit busy," Anesko said. "Is it important?"

"Extremely," Maren said, crossing the chamber and taking a seat. She looked back at me expectantly.

"She's right." I followed her lead, but remained standing. "I know where we can find more dragons."

"I appreciate what you've done to track down the black market traders, Eldwin, but we don't have the time or the resources to dedicate to taking down a safe house. My spies at the palace tell me that Erling is preparing his troops."

I glanced at Maren. Her instincts were correct. Her father *was* willing to go to war with the Order.

"I'm not talking about the traders."

Anesko's expression darkened. I'm sure he was expecting me to reveal more bad news, but this time, I was certain he would be elated.

"Explain."

"The place in my dream I told you about … it's real. It's the home to wild dragons. We can go there and bring them back."

"How do you know it's real?"

"I found a mention of it in the library, but the Assembly confirmed its existence. Tyrval is the one who was sending me the dreams, hoping I'd figure it out on my own. She said there are wild dragons there, and we need to bring them here for the survival of both our kinds."

"Our survival? What is she talking about?"

"She wouldn't explain." A thought occurred to me suddenly, and I glanced at Maren again. The full realization of what Tyrval meant finally clicked. "Wait. What if Tyrval knew what Erling was plotting? Only, what if he isn't planning to take over the Order, but to destroy it?"

"Why would he do that?" Anesko asked, though his tone implied he wasn't necessarily disbelieving of the theory.

"I can't pretend to understand Erling's mind, but clearly, he has greater plans. Maybe he's going to do something that we wouldn't allow. Something tyrannical."

The color in Maren's face disappeared.

"Eldwin's right," she said. "My father has never been satisfied with what he has. He wants more. He always has. What he might be planning, though, I do not know."

"If Erling seeks to destroy the Order, he will not find it a simple task, no matter our numbers," Anesko said. "It will take him at least a week to march his armies to our gates. That gives us some time to prepare." He looked at Katori. "I will need your help"

"You have it," she said.

"Thank you." Anesko turned his gaze back on me. "How far away are the cliffs?"

"I don't know. Tyrval told me the land is to the west, across the ocean. A few days, probably."

"If Sion was in perfect health, I'd agree. You'll need to take a ship, which is going to take longer. If Tyrval is right and you find these wild dragons, the Citadel will probably be under siege by the time you return with them."

"They'll be our salvation," I said.

"Unless they refuse to come. You must do everything in your power to convince them."

"I will."

"I don't like the idea of being even more shorthanded than we already are, but I like the idea of you traveling alone even less, especially since those slayers are still out there somewhere. We need to ensure you reach your destination. You and Maren will go together."

"Our dragons, too, right?" I asked.

"Of course. Sion may struggle to cross the ocean, but that is something you'll have to figure out when you get to the coast. Rest and prepare today. You will leave first thing in the morning. We'll lower the barrier long enough to let you out, then the Citadel will become an impenetrable fortress for as long as we can keep it that way."

The weight of the Order was on our shoulders, but for some reason, I wasn't feeling stressed. It was more a feeling of acceptance. This was the path before us, and we would see it through regardless of what awaited us.

"We'll leave you to it, then."

I held my hand out to Maren. She grabbed ahold of it, and I pulled her to her feet and kept her hand in mine as we left Anesko's office.

"I'm glad you're coming with me," I said.

"So am I. I don't like being away from you."

The world might be about to burn down, but as long as I had Maren and Sion, I would face the flames without fear.

14

Night fell, but things around the Citadel weren't much different from normal. The atmosphere among the other riders was upbeat. I assumed no one wanted to dwell on the approaching darkness, and I didn't blame them. Everything we knew was at risk of being destroyed, all because the king was a fool.

I pushed the negative thoughts away and tried to enjoy what might be my last night in the Citadel. Dinner was a lavish affair, with the kitchen staff serving exotic desserts and a host of other foods we rarely saw. I ate until I felt so full my stomach would burst, and then Maren and I retired to our room for the night.

As we lay in bed, I ran my fingers through her red hair and pondered what the world would be like when we had children. It was possible we wouldn't survive Erling's wrath, but I refused to believe that. And he wouldn't kill his own daughter, would he?

I eventually fell asleep, and that last thought must have stayed in my subconscious, for my dreams were full of battles and death, including Maren's. I awoke drenched in sweat, but when I realized it was only a dream, my racing heart calmed and I went back to sleep. The nightmares didn't return, but my rest was fitful and I continuously woke up for no reason.

When dawn arrived, I felt more tired than the previous day. Despite that, I was somewhat excited. Maren and I would be the first people to travel across the ocean to find wild dragons, and the potential that brought was enough to drown out my worries.

I wasn't hungry, so I skipped breakfast and instead gathered the supplies we would need for our journey. I packed two bags with food and canteens to ensure we didn't have to ration anything. Since we would have to book passage on a ship, I assumed we could restock our supplies before sailing off. That, or the ship would have what we needed on board. As I was taking the bags to the stable, I passed Curate Henrik in the hall.

"Master Anesko asked for you to come see him before you depart," he said.

"Thanks. I'll drop these off and head there when I'm done."

"Stay safe out there. A lot is going on, so don't let your guard down."

"I don't plan to. Try to keep this place in one piece while I'm gone. I'd hate to come back to a pile of rubble."

Henrik and I chuckled, but there was a level of seriousness beneath my words. I continued to the stable and left Maren's bag outside Demris's cave, then entered Sion's and strapped my bag to her saddle.

How are you feeling? I asked.

Better. Are we going somewhere?

You didn't read my thoughts? You always do.

I was asleep, Sion replied. *What did I miss?*

We're going to find the wild dragons. If you don't think you can make it, Demris can take us both.

Sion rumbled her displeasure.

Don't be silly. I'm always ready for adventure.

And that's usually what gets you into trouble.

Is there an update on the situation with Erling?

Not much since yesterday. Anesko's spies confirmed the king's armies are preparing to march.

Perhaps the king is bluffing. It could be nothing more than a show of force.

That would be great, but I doubt it, I said. I'm confident his goal is to destroy the Order and every one part of it.

He will find dragons are formidable foes. We will not go down before burning his armies to ash.

I smiled and patted her neck.

One obstacle at a time. First, we need to reach the coast. As long as Erling doesn't have any scouts hanging around, it should be an easy trip.

Demris and I will be extra vigilant, Sion said.

Good. Make sure you eat before we leave. I'd like to make as few stops as possible.

I finished my meal just before you arrived. The guards delivered an extra helping of sheep.

Sion hummed, her appreciation filling the bond.

I'll return shortly.

I went back inside the school and made my way to Anesko's office. His door was open, and I found him seated behind his desk. Normally, he'd be rifling through reports, but he was leaning back in his chair, arms folded across his chest.

"You wanted to see me?" I asked.

"Yes. Since you need a ship, you will need money." He leaned forward and opened one of the desk drawers, fishing a coin purse out. It clinked as he set it on the desk. "Try not to lose it."

I took the purse and emptied the coins into my hand, then deposited them into my own purse and laid the empty one on the desk.

"I didn't lose the king's money," I said. "I used it to pay my contact in Ilok."

"It was a joke, Eldwin. I was never worried about you paying the king back. It was a paltry sum for him."

I nodded, figuring as much.

"We'll return as soon as possible."

"I'll be here," Anesko said, cracking a smile. "Waiting for good news, if all goes well."

"Maren and I will do everything possible to come back with an army of dragons."

"I hope that is the case. You should get going. Every moment you spend here is another Erling's armies draw closer."

"Thank you for entrusting me with this. I'll see you soon."

"Goodbye, Eldwin."

I left his office, and his farewell haunted me. I prayed this would not be the last time I saw him. Maren was in the dining hall eating breakfast, so I took my time walking there. She was a completely different person when she was hungry, and I didn't want to deal with her alter ego on this trip.

She was stepping into the hall as I arrived, and I fell into step beside her and placed my arm across her shoulders, pulling her close as we walked.

"The bags are in the stable and Sion is feeling rested, so we're all set."

"Did you eat?" Maren asked.

"I'm still full from dinner," I replied. "I'll be fine for a few hours. I can eat later."

"If you say so."

We stopped by our room to grab a traveling cloak for Maren, then we headed down to the stable and temporarily parted ways. I climbed up Sion's shoulder, leaning forward in the saddle to keep from hitting my head on the ceiling. Once Sion stepped out into the courtyard, I sat up straight and looked at the magical barrier that glowed faintly around the border of the Citadel. Demris and Maren quickly joined us, and I looked over at her.

"How long do you think the barrier will hold?"

"Until the sorcerers sustaining it fall from exhaustion or death. They are working in shifts to keep the strain to a minimum, but once it's being used to deflect attacks, it will take every one of them to keep it in place."

Magic could be used for good or for ill, and the more I learned about it, the more I wished I could use it. I waved at one of the guards until I got his attention, then pointed to the barrier. He nodded and rushed off. A few moments later, the barrier where we were rippled, and a portion of it faded from existence.

Let's go, I told Sion, and she leaped into the air. Demris followed us, and once both dragons cleared the walls, the hole in the barrier closed. I stared back at the Citadel for a moment, then turned my gaze ahead.

Take us west.

15

We flew for hours before Sion needed to rest. It surprised me she'd recovered enough to go as far as she did, and we landed at the base of the Wintersor Mountains. She lay like a cat, her tail tucked around her body. I looked up at the peaks and wondered how the people of Valgaard were doing with Hrodin gone. His decision to side with Kage had sealed his fate, and I still did not know what the Assembly did with him other than they had locked him up.

"This brings back memories, doesn't it?" I asked, looking at Maren.

She nodded, but she wasn't staring at the mountains. She was looking west.

"This is the farthest we've been in this direction," she said, changing the subject. "I've never given it much thought, but now that I think about it, I am curious to see what lies this way. This is the fringe of Osnen."

"I've never heard of any riders going out this far, so it can't be very populated."

"Maybe Valgaard watches over this portion of Osnen?"

"That's true. I hadn't considered that."

I looked back the way we'd come, scanning the sky. There was no sign of pursuit, so the king must not have left any scouts around the Citadel. Things were going well so far in that regard, but we still had the slayers to worry about.

They have a distinct presence, Sion said. *Now that we've encountered them in person, I'll have a better sense of their approach, especially since their movements won't be concealed by magic.*

We know little about them, so we shouldn't discount that they may have other magic users among them.

A wise observation.

Stay alert and don't get too comfortable, I said. *Until we're out on the water, we're still in danger of running into them.*

Dragons are always alert, Sion huffed.

I smiled and rubbed her snout. *You know what I mean.*

I opened the bag on Sion's saddle and withdrew some of the food I'd packed. A few pieces of dried meat and a slice of yellow cheese would hold me over until dinner. Hopefully, we'd be at our destination by then.

It shouldn't be much farther. I can smell water in the air.

I hope you're right. It would be great if we could return with the wild dragons before Erling arrives at the Citadel.

Given our history with plans, I wouldn't count on things going easy.

Don't remind me, I said.

I ate in silence and surveyed the landscape, enjoying its untamed beauty. After half an hour, Sion stood and stretched her wings.

I am ready to fly again.

"Time to go," I told Maren.

She was lying in the grass beside Demris, hands underneath her head and eyes closed against the sun. She got up and brushed herself off. We mounted up and set off again. The mountains eventually turned to hills, which turned into flat grassland. There were no settlements that I could see, and I wondered if there was any civilization out here at all.

On the horizon, I could see the ocean. It stretched on and on with no end in sight. As we drew closer, a town came into view. It had a port and there were several ships anchored. I took that as a good sign.

We landed on the outskirts of the city, and Maren and I continued on foot. We didn't know if the Order's presence here was viewed as unfavorably as other places, and I figured it was best to investigate first rather than make any assumptions. There were no walls or gates prohibiting entrance, and we walked into the boundary of the city unimpeded. The usual sounds of city life were absent, and I didn't see many people.

"Seems abandoned," I whispered.

"Not completely, but where did everyone go?

This place isn't exactly small."

"I didn't see any other settlements on the way. Maybe something caused the people that used to be here to leave."

"Maybe."

The buildings were in ill repair, and the streets were overgrown with weeds that had found life in the cracks between the cobblestones. I saw an elderly man sitting on the stairs of a small house, his gnarled hands repairing a fishing net. He paused to look at us curiously for a moment, then went back to work.

The principal thoroughfare took us down to the docks, and I stopped mid-step. Maren also stopped. The ships weren't anchored in the harbor. They were sunk, only the top portions visible above the water. The wood on all of them was rotted, which indicated they had been this way for a long time.

"Well, I wasn't expecting this."

"Me neither," I said. I looked down the entire harbor and noticed one ship wasn't sunk, but its condition didn't look much better than those that were. "Look there."

"It's a sliver of hope."

"Sometimes that's all you need. Come on."

I led the way to the ship, leaving the solid ground behind and traversing the dock. Although it was a solid walkway, the fact it was built on the water and no one appeared to be doing any upkeep on it made me a little wary.

We reached the wharf where the ship was docked and I spotted a barefoot man sitting on a barrel. He was shirtless and in his hand was a clear bottle with an amber liquid, which I assumed was some sort of alcohol. He looked up as we approached and offered us a toothless grin. A few days' worth of unshaven stubble covered his cheeks and jawline, and his eyes were bloodshot. He was bald, and several gold circular earrings adorned his darkly tanned skin.

"Ho there," he greeted.

"Are you the captain of this ship?"

"Sure as the sun shines. How can I help ye?"

"We're looking to book passage," I said.

"Where ye going?"

"West."

The man chuckled and took a drink from his bottle. "There's nothin' west o' here, me boy. Nothin' but dark waters."

"Well, maybe you'll be the first to find out otherwise. We need to sail west, and we have money to pay."

"Are yer coins gold?"

I reached into my purse and grabbed a handful of the coins Anesko had given me, my eyes scanning the ship to make sure it wasn't a trap. I didn't see anyone, so I pulled my hand out and spread my fingers wide to show him the coins. One slid off my palm and thudded against the walkway before rolling in between the planks and disappearing with a tiny splash. I quickly closed my hand to keep from dropping any more of them.

"The sea loves gold as much as any o' us," the captain said. "Consider it a gift to 'er."

"Will you take us?" Maren asked.

The man looked from me to Maren several times, then took a long swig from his bottle.

"Just the two o' ye?"

We both nodded.

"Well, our dragons will come, too, but they'll be flying."

"Dragons?" The captain looked up at the sky as if searching for them.

"Yes. Mine was recently injured, so if she needs to rest, is your ship able to hold her weight for a short time?"

"Afraid not, me boy. This lass doesn't have the strength for anythin' like that. Not these days."

I can swim, Sion said.

I don't know why I hadn't considered that before.

"That's all right. Just me and my wife here, then. Will you take us out there?"

"Do ye plan on comin' back?"

"Yes," I answered.

The captain stood up and ran his right hand across his sweaty scalp, then downed the rest of the liquid in the bottle and slid it into the sash around his waist.

"I think yer crazy, but I like crazy. Sailin' anywhere, even if it be nowhere, is better than bein' on land. I'll take ya, but ye'll have to help man the ship. I'm a bit short o' hands."

"We don't mind helping," Maren said.

"Good. Have ye been on a ship afore?"

"We've been on a ferry," I answered.

"Bah, that's a boat, me boy. A small boat. This here's a ship. I'll teach ye what ye need to know to be useful." The captain looked down at the water. "The tide will be comin' in soon, and then we can sail. If ye be needin' anythin' before we go, now's the time to get it."

I looked at Maren. She shook her head.

"Our dragons are carrying everything we need. I think we're all set."

"My name's Malin, but ye'll address me as cap'n."

"Yes, captain."

"I like quick learners. What do I call the two o' ye?" He smiled wide, and I saw he did have a few teeth left in his mouth.

"I'm Eldwin, and this is Maren."

"Pleased to meet ye," Malin said. "Climb

aboard."

We've got a ship, I told Sion. *Rest for now. When the tide comes in, we're setting off.*

The gangplank was wobbly, but I boarded the boat without too much trouble. I offered my hand to Maren as she reached the top and pulled her the rest of the way. The sails attached to the mast were furled, and other than a few barrels, the deck of the ship was empty.

I walked to the bow of the ship and looked out at the ocean. The first twenty feet of the water was a muddy brown, but then the water darkened, turning black as night.

"You need to see this," I called out to Maren.

She joined me at the bow and scrunched her face. "The water is black?"

I nodded. "I guess Malin wasn't kidding when he said there was nothing but dark water out there."

"Let's hope that isn't a sign of things to come," Maren said.

Tyrval hadn't led me astray yet, so I didn't see why she would now. If she said there was land out there, then I had to believe she was right.

The fate of the Citadel, of the entire Order, depended on it.

THE END OF BOOK 12

ABOUT THE AUTHOR

Richard Fierce is a fantasy and space opera author. He's been writing since childhood, but began publishing in 2007. Since then, he's written multiple novels and short stories.

In 2000, Richard won Poet of the Year for his poem *The Darkness*. He's also one of the creative brains behind the Allatoona Book Festival, a literary event in Acworth, Georgia.

A recovering retail worker, he now works in the tech industry when he's not busy writing.

He's married and has three step-daughters (pray for him), three dogs (huskies!), a cat, and two ferrets. He basically has a zoo.

His love affair with fantasy was born in high school when a friend's mother gave him a copy of *Dragons of Spring Dawning* by Margaret Weis and Tracy Hickman.